FAMILIES

POEMS CELEBRATING THE AFRICAN AMERICAN EXPERIENCE

FAMILIES

POEMS CELEBRATING THE AFRICAN AMERICAN EXPERIENCE

Selected by
Dorothy S. Strickland *and*
Michael R. Strickland

Illustrations by
John Ward

WORDSONG
Boyds Mills Press

Dedicated with love to our family —
Maurice,
Mark, and Kimberly,
Randy, Cindia, and Chelsea,
and
to the number one member of our extended family,
Bernice Cullinan

—D.S.S. & M.R.S.

Text copyright © 1994 by
Dorothy S. Strickland and Michael R. Strickland
Illustrations copyright © 1994 by John Ward

Published by Wordsong
Boyds Mills Press, Inc.
A Highlights Company
815 Church Street
Honesdale, Pennsylvania 18431
Printed in Mexico

Publisher Cataloging-in-Publication Data
Main entry under title.
    Families : poems for young children / selected by Dorothy S. Strickland and
Michael R. Strickland ; illustrated by John Ward. — 1st ed.
[32]p. : col. ill. ; cm.
Summary : Family relationships are explored and affirmed in this anthology of poems
celebrating the diversity of African American families. Works by Gwendolyn Brooks,
Lucille Clifton, and Langston Hughes are among those included.
Hardcover ISBN 1-56397-288-3 Paperback ISBN 1-56397-560-2
1. Afro-Americans—Juvenile poetry. 2. Children's poetry, American.
[1. Afro-Americans—Poetry. 2. American poetry.] I. Strickland, Dorothy S.
II. Strickland, Michael R. III. Ward, John, ill. IV. Title.
811.008—dc20   1994
Library of Congress Catalog Card Number 93-61162

Book designed by Charlotte Staub
The text of this book is set in 16-point Cochin.
The illustrations are done in acrylics.

Hardcover 10 9 8 7 6 5 4
Paperback 10 9 8 7 6 5 4

Permission to reprint previously published material
may be found on page 31.

FAMILIES, FAMILIES
All kinds of families.
Mommies and daddies,
Sisters and brothers,
Aunties and uncles,
    And cousins, too.

FAMILIES, FAMILIES
All kinds of families.
People who live with us,
People who care for us,
Grandmas and grandpas,
    And babies, brand new.

FAMILIES, FAMILIES
All kinds of families.
Coming and going,
Laughing and singing,
Caring and sharing,
    And loving you.

Dorothy and Michael Strickland

CONTENTS

BLACK PARENT TO CHILD

Your world's wide open.
Walk right in.
Drown yourself with knowledge;
drench yourself with skills.
The world's wide open, child;
walk right in.

Naomi F. Faust

ANDRE

I had a dream last night. I dreamed
I had to pick a Mother out.
I had to choose a Father too.
At first, I wondered what to do,
There were so many there, it seemed,
Short and tall and thin and stout.

But just before I sprang awake,
I knew what parents I would take.

And *this* surprised and made me glad:
They were the ones I always had!

Gwendolyn Brooks

MOM IS WOW!

Mothers are finders and keepers
They are comforters of weepers
They are lullers-abye for sleepers.

Mothers are good-manners makers
They are temperature takers
They are the best of birthday bakers.
Mom is Wow!

Mothers are sick-bed sit besiders
They are hiding place providers
They are pin-the-tail guiders.

Mothers are prayer makers in the nights
They are enders of quarrels and fights
They are teachers of duties and rights.
Mom is Wow!

Julia Fields

Pretty.
That's what Daddy
says I am
whenever he comes
to get me.
I love him
and I'm glad
he's gonna come today.

Oh, I wish he'd hurry up!

Nikki Grimes

THE DRUM

daddy says the world is
a drum tight and hard
and i told him
i'm gonna beat
out my own rhythm

Nikki Giovanni

I REMEMBER

I remember
walking down the street beside
Uncle Eddie's legs
taking a nap in Mama's lap
talking to the pigeons in the park
I remember
my fuzzy hat, my yellow cat
my potty pot
I remember a lot
but I wish I remembered
what I forgot

Eloise Greenfield

HUGS AND KISSES

Hugs and hugs and kisses . . .
Doesn't she know that I'm a boy?
Hugs and hugs and kisses . . .
I'm not some cuddly toy.
Hugs and hugs and kisses . . .
Boys should be treated rough.
Hugs and hugs and kisses . . .
These muscles show I'm tough.

Hugs and hugs and kisses . . .
Makes me want to run and hide.
I can't show the world how warm
Her hugs and hugs and kisses
Makes me feel . . . inside.

Lindamichellebaron

14

AUNT SUE'S STORIES

Aunt Sue has a head full of stories.
Aunt Sue has a whole heart full of stories.
Summer nights on the front porch
Aunt Sue cuddles a brown-faced child to her bosom
And tells him stories.

Black slaves
Working in the hot sun,
And black slaves
Walking in the dewy night,
And black slaves
Singing sorrow songs on the banks of a mighty river
Mingle themselves softly
In the flow of old Aunt Sue's voice,
Mingle themselves softly
In the dark shadows that cross and recross
Aunt Sue's stories.

And the dark-faced child, listening,
Knows that Aunt Sue's stories are real stories.
He knows that Aunt Sue never got her stories
Out of any book at all,
But that they came
Right out of her own life.

The dark-faced child is quiet
Of a summer night
Listening to Aunt Sue's stories.

Langston Hughes

HONEY, I LOVE

I love
I love a lot of things, a whole lot of things
Like
My cousin comes to visit and you know he's from the South
'Cause every word he says just kind of slides out of his mouth
I like the way he whistles and I like the way he walks
But honey, let me tell you that I LOVE the way he talks
    I love the way my cousin talks
        and

The day is hot and icky and the sun sticks to my skin
Mr. Davis turns the hose on, everybody jumps right in
The water stings my stomach and I feel so nice and cool
Honey, let me tell you that I LOVE a flying pool
    I love to feel a flying pool
        and

Renee comes out to play and brings her doll without a dress
I make a dress with paper and that doll sure looks a mess
We laugh so loud and long and hard the doll falls to the ground
Honey, let me tell you that I LOVE the laughing sound
    I love to make the laughing sound
        and

My uncle's car is crowded and there's lots of food to eat
We're going down the country where the church folks like to meet
I'm looking out the window at the cows and trees outside
Honey, let me tell you that I LOVE to take a ride
I love to take a family ride

and

My mama's on the sofa sewing buttons on my coat
I go and sit beside her, I'm through playing with my boat
I hold her arm and kiss it 'cause it feels so soft and warm
Honey, let me tell you that I LOVE my mama's arm
I love to kiss my mama's arm

and

It's not so late at night, but still I'm lying in my bed
I guess I need my rest, at least that's what my mama said
She told me not to cry 'cause she don't want to hear a peep
Honey, let me tell you I DON'T love to go to sleep
I do not love to go to sleep
But I love
I love a lot of things, a whole lot of things
And honey,
I love you, too.

Eloise Greenfield

THURSDAY EVENING
BEDTIME

Afraid of the dark
is afraid of Mom
and Daddy
and Papa
and Cousin Tom.

"I'd be as silly
as I could be,
afraid of the dark
is afraid of Me!"

says ebony
Everett
Anderson.

Lucille Clifton

Big sister tells me
        that i'm black
she tries to keep me
        right on track

she says that black men must stand tall
            that man and woman
            woman and man
grow big black family
        big black plan

she says that black men must stand tall
            and we can see
                we must be free

that we are bright
with all our might

and we are strong
        to sing our song

that we are proud
we shout out loud

Arnold Adoff

AS SOON AS SHE IS UP

Grandma is up
      And
         Out   side
Picking the
Fresh
      And
         New
      And
         Tender

Dandelion greens   to
               Cook
               Up
               For
               Us
               All

Arnold Adoff

20

GO AWAY!

Somehow I'm always
                    in the way.
I'm always sent somewhere
                    to play,
Or told to go and watch tv.
Is it them?
                    Or is it me?

Lindamichellebaron

SEEING A NEW SISTER

Baby sister doesn't know
What's going on at all;
How will I ever play with her?
She is so soft and small.

How can I even talk to her?
She only sleeps and sleeps;
But I suppose we'll get along —
They say she's here for keeps.

E. Alma Flagg

FRIDAY
WAITING FOR MOM

When I am seven
Mama can stay
from work and play with me
all day.

I won't go to school,
I'll pull up a seat
by her and we can talk
and eat

and we will laugh
at how it ends;
Mama and
Everett Anderson —
Friends.

Lucille Clifton

MISSING MAMA

last year when Mama died
I went to my room to hide
from the hurt
I closed my door
wasn't going to come out
no more, never
but my uncle he said
you going to get past
this pain
      you going to
push on past this pain
and one of these days
you going to feel like
yourself again
I don't miss a day
remembering Mama
sometimes I cry
but mostly
I think about
the good things
now

Eloise Greenfield

MY NATURAL MAMA

my natural mama
is gingerbread
all brown and
spicy sweet.
some mamas are rye
or white or
golden wheat
but my natural mama
is gingerbread,
brown and spicy sweet.

Lucille Clifton

IN BOTH THE FAMILIES

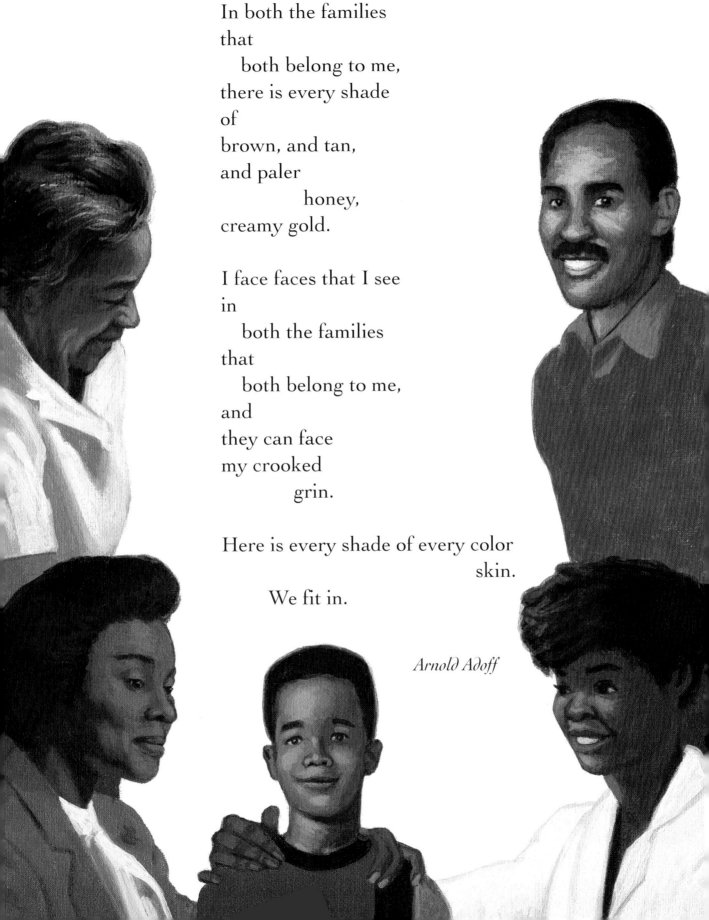

In both the families
that
    both belong to me,
there is every shade
of
brown, and tan,
and paler
            honey,
creamy gold.

I face faces that I see
in
    both the families
that
    both belong to me,
and
they can face
my crooked
        grin.

Here is every shade of every color
                        skin.

    We fit in.

Arnold Adoff

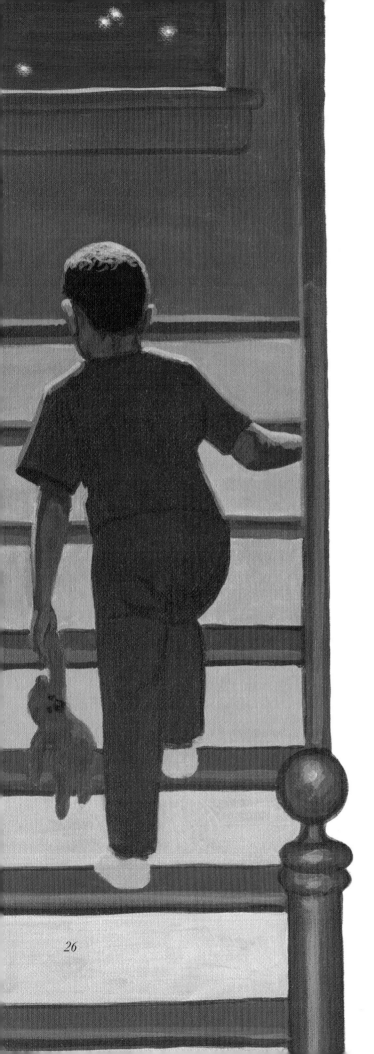

GOOD NIGHT

Goodnight Mommy
Goodnight Dad

I kiss them as I go

Goodnight Teddy
Goodnight Spot

The moonbeams call me so

I climb the stairs
Go down the hall
And walk into my room

My day of play is ending
But my night of sleep's in bloom

Nikki Giovanni

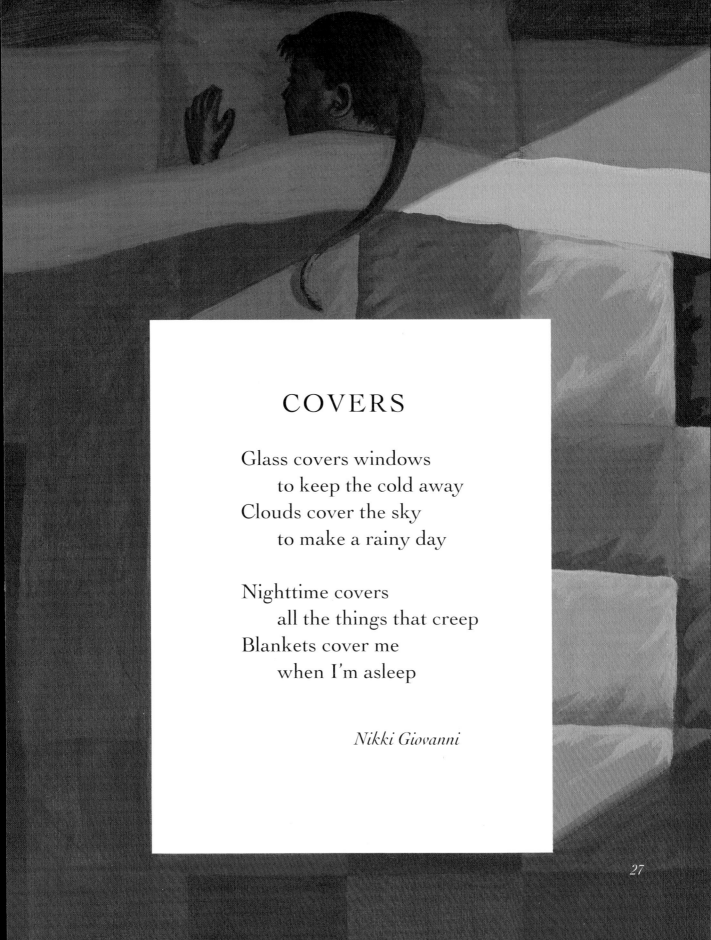

COVERS

Glass covers windows
    to keep the cold away
Clouds cover the sky
    to make a rainy day

Nighttime covers
    all the things that creep
Blankets cover me
    when I'm asleep

Nikki Giovanni

LULLABY
(For a Black Mother)

My little dark baby,
My little earth-thing,
My little love-one,
What shall I sing
For your lullaby?

Stars,
Stars,
A necklace of stars
Winding the night.

My little black baby,
My dark body's baby,
What shall I sing
For your lullaby?

Moon,
Moon,
Great diamond moon,
Kissing the night.

Oh, little dark baby,
Night black baby,

Stars, stars,
Moon,
Night stars,
Moon,

For your sleep-song lullaby!

Langston Hughes

HUSH, LITTLE BABY

Softly rocking

Lullaby

2. If that diamond ring turns brass,
   Papa's going to buy you a looking glass.

3. If that looking glass gets broke,
   Papa's going to buy you a billy goat.

4. If that billy goat won't pull,
   Papa's going to buy you a cart and bull.

5. If that cart and bull turns over,
   Papa's going to buy you a dog named Rover.

6. If that dog named Rover won't bark,
   Papa's going to buy you a horse and cart.

7. If that horse and cart fall down,
   You'll still be the sweetest baby in town!

Acknowledgments

Every effort has been made to trace the ownership of all copyrighted material and to secure the necessary permissions to reprint these selections. If any errors or omissions have occurred, corrections will be made in subsequent printings, provided that the publisher is notified of their existence.

"As Soon as She Is Up" from GREENS by Arnold Adoff. Copyright © 1988 by Arnold Adoff. "In Both the Families" from ALL THE COLORS OF THE RACE by Arnold Adoff. Copyright © 1982 by Arnold Adoff. Reprinted with permission from Lothrop, Lee & Shepard books, a division of William Morrow & Company, Inc.

"Big Sister Tells Me That I'm Black" from BIG SISTER TELLS ME THAT I'M BLACK by Arnold Adoff. Copyright © 1976 by Arnold Adoff. Reprinted with permission from Henry Holt and Company, Inc.

"Andre" from BRONZEVILLE BOYS AND GIRLS by Gwendolyn Brooks. Copyright © 1956 by Gwendolyn Brooks Blakely. Reprinted with permission from HarperCollins Publishers.

"My Natural Mama" by Lucille Clifton. Copyright © 1988 by Lucille Clifton. Reprinted with permission from Curtis Brown, Ltd.

"Friday Waiting for Mom" and "Thursday Evening Bedtime" from SOME OF THE DAYS OF EVERETT ANDERSON by Lucille Clifton. Copyright © 1970 by Lucille Clifton. Reprinted with permission from Henry Holt and Company, Inc.

"Black Parent to Child" from ALL BEAUTIFUL THINGS by Naomi F. Faust, published by Lotus Press (Detroit, Michigan). Reprinted with permission from the author.

"Mom Is Wow!" by Julia Fields. Reprinted with permission from the author.

"Seeing a New Sister" from FEELINGS, LINES, COLORS by E. Alma Flagg. Reprinted with permission from the author.

"Covers" and "Good Night" from VACATION TIME by Nikki Giovanni. Copyright © 1981 by Nikki Giovanni. Reprinted with permission from William Morrow & Company, Inc.

"the drum" from SPIN A SOFT BLACK SONG by Nikki Giovanni. Copyright © 1971 by Nikki Giovanni. Reprinted with permission from Farrar, Straus & Giroux, Inc.

"Honey I Love" from HONEY I LOVE by Eloise Greenfield. Copyright © 1978 by Eloise Greenfield. Reprinted with permission from HarperCollins Publishers.

"I Remember" and "Missing Mama" by Eloise Greenfield. Copyright © 1988 by Eloise Greenfield. Reprinted by permission of Marie Brown Associates.

"Pretty" from SOMETHING ON MY MIND by Nikki Grimes. Copyright © 1978 by Nikki Grimes. Reprinted with permission from Dial Books for Young Readers, a division of Penguin Books USA Inc.

"Aunt Sue's Stories" from SELECTED POEMS by Langston Hughes. Copyright © 1926 by Alfred A. Knopf, Inc., and renewed 1954 by Langston Hughes. Reprinted with permission from the publisher.

"Go Away!" and "Hugs and Kisses" by Lindamichellebaron. Reprinted with permission from the author.